We're Going on a Ghost Hunt

by **Susan Pearson**   illustrated by **S. D. Schindler**

SCHOLASTIC INC.

ISBN 978-0-545-65274-2

Text copyright © 2012 by Susan Pearson. Illustrations copyright © 2012 by S.D. Schindler. All rights reserved. Published by Scholastic Inc., 557 Broadway, New York, NY 10012, by arrangement with Amazon Children's Publishing. SCHOLASTIC and associated logos are trademarks and/or registered trademarks of Scholastic Inc.

12 11 10 9 8 7 6 5 4 3 2   13 14 15 16 17 18/0

Printed in the U.S.A.   08

First Scholastic printing, October 2013

The illustrations were rendered in watercolor, gouache, and colored pencil.
Book design by Vera Soki
Editor: Margery Cuyler

To Owen
—S.P.

To Eileen
—S.S.

We're going on a ghost hunt.
We're going to find a big one.
It's a starry night. The moon is bright.
We're not afraid.

Oh, no! What's this?
A muddy, murky swamp!
We can't go over it.
We can't go under it.
We'll have to go through it.

squish—
    squash—
        squoosh!

We're going on a ghost hunt.
We're going to find a big one.
It's a starry night. The moon is bright.
We're not afraid.

Oh, no! What's this?
A rustling, rattling cornfield.
We can't go over it.
We can't go under it.
We'll have to go through it.
Rustle-rustle-rat-a-tattle!

We're going on a ghost hunt.
We're going to find a big one.
It's a starry night. The moon is bright.
We're not afraid.

Oh, no! What's this?
A swishy, fishy river.
We can't go over it.
We can't go under it.
We'll have to go through it.
Do the dog paddle.
Do the back stroke.

SPLASH! SPLASH! SPLASH!

We're going on a ghost hunt.
We're going to find a big one.
It's a starry night. The moon is bright.
We're not afraid.

Oh, no! What's this?
The wild, windy woods.
We can't go over them.
We can't go under them.
We'll have to go through them.

TIPTOE . . . TIPTOE . . .

SHHHHH!

We're going on a ghost hunt.
We're going to find a big one.
It's a starry night. The moon is bright.
We're not afraid.

Oh, no! What's this?
A giant tree!
We can't go over it.
We can't go under it.
We'll have to climb up it.
What do you see?

We're going on a ghost hunt.
We're going to find a big one.
It's a starry night. The moon is bright.
We're not afraid.

Back through the gate!

creeeeak-squeeeak-EEEEEEEK!

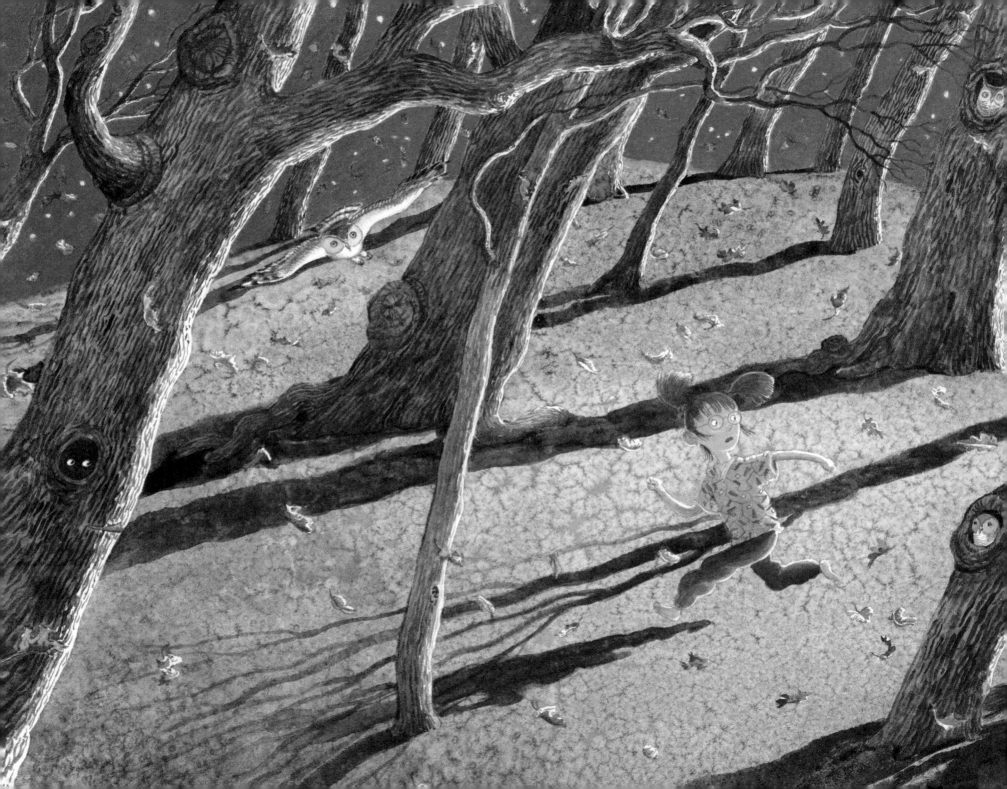

Forget the tree!
Back through the windy woods!
HOOO-HOOOOOO!
HOOOOOOOOOO!

Back through the swishy, fishy river!
Stroke, stroke—fast, fast!
Paddle, paddle—faster, faster!
SPLASH! SPLASH! SPLASH!

Back through the rustling, rattling cornfield!

Back through the muddy, murky swamp.
squish—squash—squoosh!

Back into our house,

race up the stairs,

jump into bed,
get under the covers.
Where's my teddy bear? Grab him quick!
Cuddle up close,
safe from the ghost.

Ahhhhhhhhh!
We made it!

Let's go on a ghost hunt tomorrow!